I'm a T. REX!

By Dennis R. Shealy

Illustrated by Brian Biggs

A GOLDEN BOOK · NEW YORK

Text copyright © 2010 by Dennis R. Shealy
Illustrations copyright © 2010 by Brian Biggs
All rights reserved.
Published in the United States by Golden Books, an imprint of Random House Children's Books,
a division of Random House, Inc., 1745 Broadway, New York, NY 10019.
Golden Books, A Golden Book, A Little Golden Book, the G colophon, and the distinctive
gold spine are registered trademarks of Random House, Inc.
www.randomhouse.com/kids
Educators and librarians, for a variety of teaching tools, visit us at www.randomhouse.com/kids
Library of Congress Control Number: 2009922541
ISBN: 978-0-375-85806-2
Printed in the United States of America
20 19 18 17

From the tip of my tail to the top
of my snout, there's just no doubt . . .

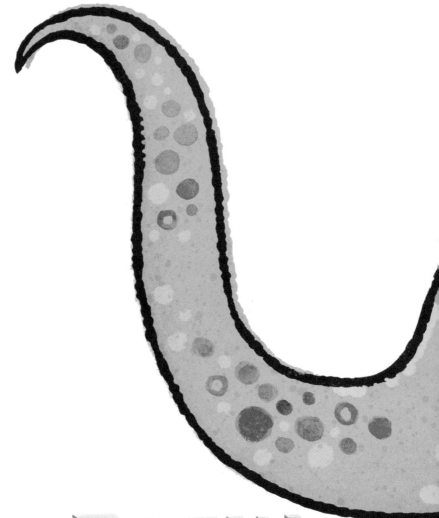

I'm a **T. REX!**

I ROARRRRR
and I romp!

I GRRROWWLLL and I stomp!

I'm a **T. REX.**

I SNARRRLLLL
and I grunt!

I prowl and I hunt!

I'm a **T. REX.**

I lived in a time called Cretaceous—
good gracious!
That just means a long time ago.

I'm *king* of the Cretaceous—that's the
rex in my name.

But *Tyrannosaurus* is a mouthful—

I'm a T. REX all the same!

Does the **T** stand for Toothy?

Does the **T** stand for Tall?

I'm big. I'm bad.
I sometimes bully,

but I like to fill
my stomach fully.

I'm a **T. REX.**

And when I'm hungry for a fresher snack—
SNAP!

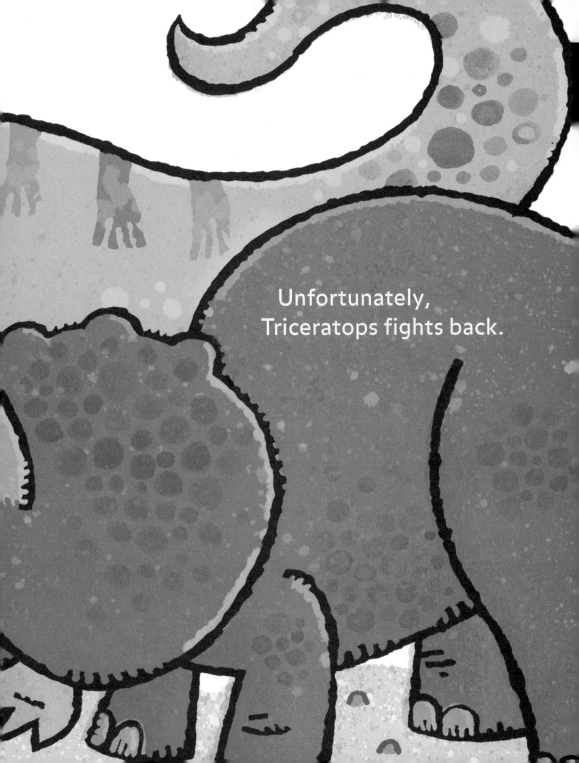

Unfortunately,
Triceratops fights back.

Giganotosaurus!

Spinosaurus!

Carcharodontosaurus!

They are all bigger—and maybe even quicker—but I just snicker.

'Cause **I'm a T. REX.**

I am fierce!

I am tall!

And I'm still the most
famous dinosaur of all.

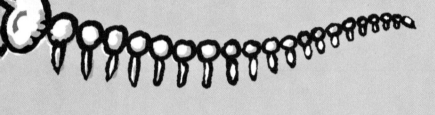

(Thank you. Thank you.
I'm a **T. REX.**)

So can you believe I started out small?
Just an egg in a nest . . .

. . . with a GREAT BIG MOMMY T. REX!

Grumpy Cat

The Little GRUMPY CAT That Wouldn't

Illustrated by **Steph Laberis**

 A GOLDEN BOOK • NEW YORK

grumpycats.com
randomhousekids.com
Educators and librarians, for a variety of teaching tools, visit us at RHTeachersLibrarians.com
ISBN 978-0-399-55354-7 (trade)—ISBN 978-0-399-55355-4 (ebook)
Printed in the United States of America
10 9 8 7 6 5 4 3 2 1

Once, there was a little cat.
She was cute. She was furry.
And she was . . .

Grumpy Cat didn't like anything.

Grumpy Cat went outside. She wanted to be alone. But soon a happy butterfly started talking to her.

Grumpy Cat didn't know the butterfly's name.

She didn't care.

"Hi, Grumpy Cat!" the butterfly said. "You know what's great about the outdoors?"

"NOTHING," Grumpy Cat said.

Grumpy Cat wanted the happy butterfly
to go away. But it didn't.
    Instead, a cheerful ladybug joined them.

"Good morning, Grumpy Cat,"
the ladybug said.

"THERE'S NO SUCH THING,"
Grumpy Cat said.

"Grumpy Cat, would you like to play?"
the butterfly asked.

Grumpy Cat wouldn't.

"Come on, it will be fun!"
the ladybug said.

"I HAD FUN ONCE," Grumpy Cat said.
"IT WAS AWFUL."

A joyful bird joined in.
Grumpy Cat was surrounded by
happy animals.

"Grumpy Cat, there must be something fun you would do," the bird said. "I know! Would you like to race?"

Would Grumpy Cat?

READY,

SET . . .

"No." Grumpy Cat wouldn't.

The happy animals all raced away.

Grumpy Cat was alone.